Advance Praise for

THE DISCUS THROWER
MEETS PETER PAN

"When our company sponsored the restoration of the Discus Thrower statue at Randall's Island Park in the late 1990s, we hoped it would serve as a symbol of New York City's strong and triumphant spirit for generations to come—and it has. Pinky Keehner's *The Discus Thrower Meets Peter Pan* is an invitation to dream, and a reminder of public art's ability to continually inspire and expand imaginations."

> — **MICHAEL R. BLOOMBERG,**
> *founder of Bloomberg LP and Bloomberg Philanthropies, and 108th mayor of New York City*

"Pinky Keehner's moxie and creativity, coupled with her enthusiasm for the transformation of Randall's Island Park, led her to write this charming tale of two iconic statues, our own Discus Thrower and our neighbor Peter Pan, and their individual evolutions."

> — **AIMEE BODEN,** *past president, Randall's Island Park Alliance (1992– 2020), and* **DEBORAH MAHER,** *president, Randall's Island Park Alliance (2020–present)*

"In this magical book, author Pinky Keehner and illustrator Cathy Oerter (who knows a thing or two about discus throwers!) combine to tell the fantasy story of two actual New York City statues, united briefly in an 'asylum' for derelict monuments, who spend a long night talking and imagining a return to their outdoor perches—the Discus Thrower after 25 years of dark isolation! The story captures the enigmatic, cockeyed, only-in-New York charm of classics such as E. B. White's *Stuart Little* and George Selden's *A Cricket in Times Square.* As Peter Pan keeps telling the anguishing Discus Thrower, 'Just believe!'"

—**ADRIAN BENEPE**, *president, Brooklyn Botanic Garden, and former New York City parks commissioner*

The author is donating her royalties from the sale of this book to the Randall's Island Park Alliance.

THE DISCUS
THROWER
MEETS
PETER PAN

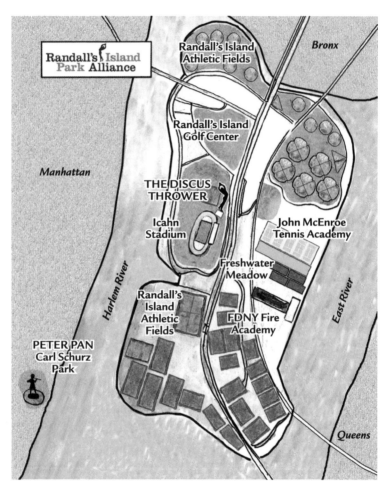

Map of Randall's Island

THE DISCUS THROWER MEETS PETER PAN

TWO NEW YORK CITY ICONS JOIN FORCES FOR SURVIVAL

By Pinky Keehner

Illustrated by
Cathy Oerter

Abbeville Press
New York   London

Design: Misha Beletsky
Layout: Julia Sedykh

First edition
10 9 8 7 6 5 4 3 2 1

ISBN 978-0-7892-1499-7

Library of Congress Cataloging-in-Publication Data available upon request

For bulk and premium sales and for text adoption procedures, write to Customer Service Manager, Abbeville Press, 655 Third Avenue, New York, NY 10017, or call 1-800-ARTBOOK.

Visit Abbeville Press online at www.abbeville.com.

To my grandchildren,
Graham, Sasha & Lydia

And to my friend
Al Oerter

*"If we strive to be
the best we can be,
we can do
some wonderful things
on this earth."*

Contents

1 *The Discus Thrower* 11

2 *Peter Pan Meets the Discus Thrower* 16

3 *Peter Pan Tells His Story* 19

4 *The Discus Thrower Tells His Story* 24

5 *The Discus Thrower's Brother* 30

6 *The Visitors* 35

7 *Peter Pan Leaves* 41

8 *Peter Pan's Journey* 46

9 *The Plan to Save The Discus Thrower* 50

10 *London—Paris—Rome* 56

11 *Athens—The Search For Brother* 59

12 *The Conversation With Brother* 64

13 *Finding the Postcard* 70

14 *Flying West, Ahead of the Sun* 73

15 *Jeff Finds the Postcard* 78

16 *A Third Discus Thrower?* 81

17   *Peter Pan Goes Home*   88

18   *The Discus Thrower Sees Sunshine*   92

19   *The Discus Thrower at the Foundry*   96

20   *The New Arm is Made*   99

21   *Welding Starts*   103

22   *The Discus Thrower Goes Home*   107

23   *The Welcome Home Party*   111

24   *Message From Brother*   114

YOUR SKETCHING PAGES   118

MEET THE STATUES   122

ACKNOWLEDGMENTS   127

ABOUT THE AUTHOR

    AND ILLUSTRATOR   128

1 • THE DISCUS THROWER

It was dark and it was still. The kind of dark which felt like a heavy weight all around him and the kind of still that echoed; both were far too familiar to him. He knew how very dark and very still the long night would be. He tried to relax, to allow his thoughts to travel back in time to a better place. This is how he endured the years of dark, still nights.

At last, the long silence was broken by a familiar sound. *Clank*. A distant light switch had been turned on, signaling that the huge garage doors would soon open; it was morning. He didn't know if it would be Scott or Tom or someone new who would open the doors, allowing a dusty ray of light to enter his space. But he knew that sooner or later another *clank* would follow, causing the endless rows of ceiling lights to cast a yellow glow as far as he could see. Then, once again, he knew he would return to the deafening silence he knew so well.

Despite the many years he had spent inside, behind the doors, he had never fully adjusted to the reality that his mornings were reduced quite simply to a *clank*, the sound of doors opening, and then a second *clank*, and nothing else.

His distant memories of mornings under the sky, of sunrises and nature's responses—the change in the wind, the feeling of warmth, and the sounds of awakening birds—provided him, even now, with momentary anticipation of *something more*.

However, this brief bustle of activity signaling daybreak as he now knew it would most likely be the sum and total of the action he would experience the entire day—that is, until it was replayed in reverse hours later.

He glanced from side to side and saw his neighbors just where he knew they would be. They had been his sole companions for many years. To his right, the World War I Infantry Fighter stood prepared for action; on his left perched the pair of eagles, ready to soar through the air; and straight ahead a group of Victorian lampposts were poised to shine their light into the vast darkness.

But none of them had the power to do so. It was an odd assortment. Singly, they each referenced a special time in history, but huddled together they made no sense at all. It was as if a vortex had randomly yanked them from their places and deposited them at his side.

He didn't know what else went on in other parts of the building. His life was limited to only one section of this sprawling floor, although occasionally people would walk by and look through the thick wire screen that enclosed him like a cage.

But as fit and handsome as he once was, they no longer paused to admire him—his powerful body, his classic profile, his elegant grace. There had been a time when all eyes were on him, when he would even look away, not wanting to engage anyone, determined not to be diverted from his goal of becoming the best discus thrower in the world. But now he yearned to be the focus of an appreciative glance once again.

Rarely, very rarely indeed, but once in a while, someone would actually unlock the padlock on the huge chain and swing back one of the doors, causing him great anxiety and concern. He would vacillate between hoping that he was the reason for the visit and praying that he was not, between hoping that at last he would be rescued and fearing that he had been deemed worthless after all and would be scrapped. He was prepared to go anywhere now, though for years he had wished only to return to Greece.

But now anywhere outside would be welcome so that he might again feel the sun on his back and hear the sounds of the street and just perhaps be the object of a pair of admiring eyes.

2 • PETER PAN MEETS THE DISCUS THROWER

B ut this morning was different. The clanks were followed by activity, strange sounds that alarmed him. Something was about to happen. He heard voices in the distance, and as they got closer, he heard the sound of wheels squeaking on the cement floor.

He listened carefully, trying to catch a word, to get a clue as to what was coming. Someone approached the cage and removed the heavy metal lock and chain, and flung both cage doors open. He braced himself. He was both excited and scared once again. Two open doors meant only one thing: something really large was either coming into the cage . . . or leaving it.

He peered around the corner as far as he could and held his breath in anticipation. Finally, he saw a mysterious object coming toward him. High up in the air was a huge silver hook with a chain suspended from it.

Hanging from the chain was a large object swinging in the air. And then he saw the hood of the lift truck. Whatever it was, it was slowly getting closer and closer.

A few workmen accompanied the moving object. One entered the cage carrying a wooden platform and placed it on the floor. The lift truck followed and stopped so that the hook and suspended object dangled directly over the platform.

The hook gradually lowered until the object rested on the platform. It rocked back and forth, and finally it was still. The hook and chain were removed, the lift truck backed away, and then quite unceremoniously everyone left just as abruptly as they had arrived, locking the cage behind them. It was silent once again.

He strained to look at the object that lay close to his feet. Though it was right in front of him, next to the lampposts, it was hard to see who his new neighbor was. All he could make out was a long, narrow form and, at the end closest to him, something that looked like a hat.

Several people stopped by during the day to look in through the cage, and twice someone came with a hose and sprayed the mysterious object with water. This was quite odd. He had never seen this before. He reflected on the day he had arrived at the cage, a day that he remembered vividly.

He had been lowered directly onto the cement floor and left there. No spray of water, no wooden platform. It was a day he didn't like to think about but could never forget. He had not moved even an inch since then.

3 • PETER PAN
TELLS HIS STORY

lank. It was the end of the day. Suddenly it was dark again.

"Is anyone there?" asked a strange, thin voice.

"Yes, I am," the Discus Thrower replied.

"I am so afraid. I don't know what happened. Can you tell me where I am?"

"You are in a cage," he replied.

"Oh no, I can't be in a cage: I am made to fly. I have never been in a cage."

"Neither had I, once. Where were you before this?"

"Where was I? Well, everyone knows where I was! I am Peter Pan, and I was in Carl Schurz Park where the children come to play."

"I never heard of you, Peter Pan," he said. "Who do you think you are?"

"What? You gotta be kidding. I can't believe there is anyone who doesn't know who I am, particularly someone who speaks like you do, sort of educated, if I must say. But since you have clearly been living under a rock here, I'll clue you in. I am the most favorite of all children's stories. I have a most wonderful life because I can fly, and I can go to Neverland whenever I want to. I don't have to grow up and work or go to school or do what anyone tells me. I never grew up, and every child in the world wants to be just like me."

Whatever is he talking about? the Discus Thrower wondered. "Goodness," he said eventually. "That sounds like a frightful life, totally lacking in discipline and learning and self-improvement and devoid of any notion of achieving goals. How could you tolerate such an existence?"

"Hey, pal, I am—or was until just a few days ago—quite happy with my life. You don't need goals and learning, and certainly you don't need discipline when you have a bunny and a deer and a frog and Tinker Bell to lead you just where you want to go. And, if there's a problem, I simply fly away."

This discussion was so lacking in any reality that the Discus Thrower was tempted to cut it off. But then he realized that this conversation was the only one he had had in about 25 years. He decided to be patient with his new, though naive and un-sophisticated roommate.

"So, what happened to your perfect life? How did you get here?" the Discus Thrower asked.

"I really can't remember very much; all I know is that I miss my friends terribly. It happened a night ago. I was looking at the sky, watching the bright-est stars shine and thinking of which one I would fly to next, when suddenly I began to shake back and forth quite violently. The next thing I knew, I was falling sideways and bouncing down a street, and I was scared.

"And then I was lifted up and set on something like a wall or something high up and for a moment I rocked back and forth again but this time dangerously, and then . . . and then . . . it happened so quickly and was so terrible. I began falling, and I didn't know where I was going. I crashed into the water! It was dark and cold, and I kept sinking deeper and deeper.

"Suddenly I remembered that I could fly, so I tried to fly out of there, but I couldn't. It was horrible. I just kept sinking and being unable to fly away, and then I hit the bottom. It was mushy and smelly, and I couldn't even see my hand." He sniffled again.

"Well, I didn't know what to do. I had never been in such a situation. I tried all my secret powers, and nothing worked. So, I began to dream. I dreamed that Tinker Bell would find me and rescue me. And at last, my dream came true. I got out of that awful water, and now I'm here. So, tell me about you. Are you hoping Tinker Bell rescues you, too?"

4 • THE DISCUS THROWER TELLS HIS STORY

Of course not. I can't imagine having a friend named Tinker Bell, and I certainly don't fly," he told Peter Pan.

"That's odd. Who are you?"

"I am an athlete. I am the Discus Thrower." There was a long pause.

"The what?"

"*The Discus Thrower*," he replied with a touch of annoyance in his voice at Peter Pan's ignorance.

"I have never heard of a discus thrower. And, please, don't think I am stupid even though I never went to school.

"I live in a park, and I know everything there is to know about athletes and what they do—about baseball, hockey, soccer, basketball, and football. I certainly know about Jesse Owens, Pelé, Muhammad Ali, Billie Jean King, Jackie Robinson, Michael Jordan, and Tom Brady. Who ever heard of a discus thrower?"

"My friend, I am an Olympian from Athens, in Greece, the grandest of all civilizations. The ancient Greeks started the Olympics in 776 BC in Olympia. The discus was part of the pentathlon in the Ancient Olympics."

"Wow," muttered Peter Pan. "This guy's got a real big problem."

"I hate to break it to you, pal, but nobody knows about you. I can't even follow you. Who ever heard of the ancient Greeks? If you think you're so great, why don't you play a sport like baseball and hit home runs with the Yankees or the Mets?"

The Discus Thrower realized he would have to start at the very beginning with his new and quite adolescent neighbor Peter Pan. He recalled that Pan was the name of the mischievous Greek god of the woodlands, and he wondered for a moment if perhaps his new acquaintance was in fact the renegade Pan.

"Peter Pan, these sports you talk about are simply contrived variations of the original games, which included discus throwing as well as running, long jump, javelin, boxing, and wrestling. I was a contender in the modern Olympic Games, where discus throwing is also an event. The modern Olympics were founded more than a century ago in 1896 at Athens. Discus throwing is pure art. It is considered the classic athletic event."

Peter Pan rolled his eyes and murmured to himself, "This guy is nuts; it's time to get out of here." But for once he didn't have the power to get out.

"OK," he said, resigned to hearing more of the tale. "What makes you so special? What is this discus throwing anyway?"

"The discus," his friend began, "was originally made of stone, iron, bronze, or lead and is shaped like a flying saucer."

That got Peter Pan's attention: a flying saucer? He wanted to ask if it was like playing Frisbee, but before he had a chance, the lecture continued.

"The discus has changed over the years, and now it weighs about 4½ pounds, is 8½ inches in diameter, and is made of wood with a metal rim. It is solely propelled by the hand, not by a bat or stick or racket. To throw it, one must gather speed to provide the acceleration needed to hurl it as far as possible.

"The best way to do this is to whirl around and around with the arm holding the discus extended, but you must stay within the designated circle.

"Then, after two rotations, the discus is flung out in the direction of the competitive field. Controlling the discus—which is held against the hand and wrist by nothing but centrifugal force— is very difficult. Do you understand now?"

Peter Pan wanted to fly away more than ever. *What the heck is centrifugal force?* But, he reminded himself, he didn't really care. After all, he never studied anything, so why would he want to know about some kind of force when he had the best force in the world—the ability to fly? "Yah," he replied. "Got it."

"Therefore, the thrower must pivot around as fast as he can until he releases the discus."

Again, Peter Pan was interested. "Neat, you must get real dizzy doing that!"

"That's the problem, because if you get dizzy, you might lose your balance and step outside the circle, and then you would be disqualified. Or you might lose your balance and throw the discus the wrong direction. You must always know just where you are within the boundaries of the circle and the direction of the field and not get lost in the whirling. You must maintain control after releasing the discus to keep from stepping outside the circle.

"It requires a unique combination of grace, power, and concentration. In fact, the Greeks considered the rhythm and precision of an athlete throwing the discus just as important as his strength."

"So," cut in Peter Pan, "you woke up one morning, found a discus, and started to twirl around and throw it?"

"Hardly, young man. Just like you didn't simply wake up one morning and fly out the window. It takes hours and hours of practice and exercise."

"I never practiced or exercised to learn how to fly. I just woke up one morning, saw Tinker Bell, and followed her out the window."

The Discus Thrower didn't quite know how to respond to this. He decided to press on and ignored him.

"My twin brother and I began training to enter the Olympics as discus throwers when we were about 15 years old. We exercised several hours each day to build muscle in our arms and legs. We took dance classes to improve our balance."

5 • THE DISCUS
THROWER'S BROTHER

S o, how come you are in this cage? If you are so strong and courageous, why are you stuck in here?" Peter Pan, still lying on the wooden platform in front of the Discus Thrower, could not see his mighty cage-mate and had no idea what he looked like.

"I have lost my arm," the Discus Thrower said with sadness. It was the first time he had uttered those words. "I lost my arm and my discus, and I've been in this cage for 25 years."

Peter Pan didn't know what to say. Twenty-five years is a very long time to be stuck in such a terrible place. He waited a moment before asking his next question.

"Don't you want to get out of here?"

"Yes, but you must understand that things change. Life doesn't just stand still: you won't always be this age and doing the same thing. You will change and the situation around you will change, too, and you will have to adjust to these changes."

"No, my life can't change," Peter Pan protested. "I don't want it to change. I never want to be anything but who I am right now. I certainly won't grow up." And then he asked, "So, you adjusted to the change, but does that mean you aren't angry about where you are? Is being in this cage OK with you?"

"Yes, it is for now, and when the time is right, I will get out."

"So, you have no plans to escape?"

"I believe that all my years of training, my strength, my faith, and my persistence will eventually provide me with a new arm and discus, and then I will get out."

"But nothing's happened for 25 years," protested Peter Pan, stating what he thought was obvious. "I hate to tell you this, you seem like a smart guy, but your plan isn't working. You need to come up with something better or you aren't ever going to get out. You better start believing in a fairy like Tinker Bell and that somehow she'll get you out when she gets me out. You must believe!" Peter Pan struggled to be well-mannered. It took all his control not to scream out, "Get real. Pal."

"I am content in this moment; I have faith. Life has its ups and downs, and there is more for me to do here, like work harder on my strength and resolve. I am learning quite a bit even after all these years."

"This guy really is nuts to believe this stuff," muttered Peter Pan to himself as he yawned. It was very late, and he was tired. But he had one more question. The Discus Thrower said he had a twin brother. Peter Pan had no idea about brothers and sisters, or mothers and fathers. He was curious.

"What is your brother like, and where is he?"

"He looks just like me and is as strong as I am. In competition, though, I always beat him. He challenged me constantly when we were kids. I think that the rivalry between us made me work even harder, even when I wanted to quit. I never competed against anyone as tough as my brother."

"Where is he now?"

"He is in Athens, Greece, in the Zappeion Gardens in front of the Panathenaic Stadium."

Peter Pan had never heard of that place, but he didn't ask any more questions. Suddenly, it was very quiet. It was his first night in the cage, and his new friend, the ultimate athlete, or so he seemed to consider himself, had given him a lot to think about. He was pretty weird, Peter Pan concluded.

Wait 'til I tell Tink about this guy, he thought as he started to fall asleep.

But the Discus Thrower couldn't sleep. His usual calm tempo had been seriously jarred by his new, young friend's philosophy. He was sure there was no truth to it, believing in Tinker Bells and other fantasies. The wisdom of dreamers had never appealed to his own pragmatic respect for the disciplined work ethic that had successfully guided his life.

But after trying to deny that this cocky character's ramblings had any merit, he had to admit that Peter Pan had a point. After 25 years, he had made absolutely no progress.

6 • THE VISITORS

So," said a chipper and rested Peter Pan the next morning, "what shall we do today after we get out of here?"

"What makes you think we are getting out of here today?"

"Didn't you hear her? Tinker Bell came and told me. Surely, you would have heard her. You must be a very sound sleeper. She flew around all night and made quite a racket checking this place out."

"Actually, I think I was awake most of the night," the Discus Thrower said, wanting to catch Peter Pan in what was an obvious lie. He knew no one had "flown around" last night.

But Peter Pan dismissed this. "If you had been awake last night, you would surely have seen her, and I wish you had. Unless you don't believe in her—that's the only way you wouldn't have seen her. And I already told you that you MUST believe."

The Discus Thrower was at a loss for words. He had no idea how to talk to such a dreamer named Peter Pan who talked about a fairy named Tinker Bell as if she were real. He could think of nothing to say. Suddenly the sound of voices jarred him back to reality, as it had yesterday. The voices were coming closer.

"What time is the Peter Pan appointment?" Tom asked.

"Ten o'clock. Jeff wants to look at the Discus Thrower also," said Scott.

The Discus Thrower was stunned. He heard the opening of the lock, the banging of the chain as it fell, and the squeak of the cage gate as it swung back. Scott and Tom and a few strangers walked into the cage. They stopped in front of Peter Pan and knelt to look at him.

"So," asked someone the Discus Thrower assumed was Jeff, "what's the matter with our friend Peter Pan?"

The Discus Thrower was amazed that the man seemed to know Peter Pan. "I see you've been flushing him with water," Jeff said. "That's good, it helps get rid of the salt water, and it's important to do that immediately. Look at these bubbles. There is still more salt water surfacing. Unfortunately, some of the patina has eroded already. OK, let's stand him up and see how he is."

The Discus Thrower waited anxiously, knowing he would soon get a better view of his roommate. Scott and Tom shuffled around to one end of Peter Pan, the end that seemed to have a hat on it, and slowly lifted him up as water poured out around him.

When he was finally standing, his back was toward the Discus Thrower, and his hat was just below the Discus Thrower's waist. The Discus Thrower couldn't see his face, only the back of his head and hat, but he did notice that he was holding a horn that was packed with chewed bubble gum. *How disgusting*, he thought.

"OK, let's see what's happened to him," Jeff said, studying his patient. "Looks like a scrape on his knee, he's missing the top of his feather, the deer's nose is scraped, and there are a few dents. Not bad considering what happened. We can get him back in shape quickly, clean him up, and restore his color. It's not a big job. Where's the base he stood on?"

"It's that granite piece over there," said Tom.

"Eddie, come look at this," Jeff said, and everyone went to the side of the cage to see the six-sided, one-foot-thick granite slab base.

"Just a few chips missing, fortunately," Eddie said. "We need to replace the screws and iron slats which held him in place, also."

"I know you have a donor who wants the work done quickly," said Jeff. "We'll put Peter Pan on a fast track. We've got to get him back to his friends. I'll get you an estimate soon. I've also been asked to look at this guy while I'm here." He motioned toward the Discus Thrower. "It looks like he's been here for a while."

Jeff moved toward the Discus Thrower and took out a measuring tape.

"Eddie, can you take down some measurements?" Eddie took out a pencil and notebook. Jeff continued, "He is 84 inches tall. The base plate cover is 33½ by 45½ inches. He's in pretty poor condition. Original joints are beginning to open. Copper compounds have developed, not surprisingly. His left arm was cut off about 4 inches above the elbow joint. It needs to be replaced, and the discus too."

The Discus Thrower was embarrassed. He was not used to this kind of attention. He had once prided himself on his physical form, but now, in his current condition, vanity prevented his having any interest in being in the spotlight. They walked around him several times, touching him here and there. He was glad when at last they left.

7 • PETER PAN LEAVES

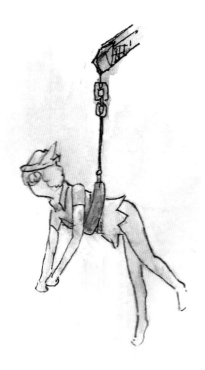

P eter Pan waited until the visitors had left
and then whispered, "See, I told you so.
We're getting out of here!"

The Discus Thrower said nothing. He was hoping
for silence so he could reflect on what had just
happened and perhaps regain a little composure.
But Peter Pan was oblivious to his feelings and
pressed on.

"So, are you left-handed, or right?" Peter Pan asked.

"Right-handed," he replied.

"Then why is it such a big deal that you lost your left arm? Don't you throw the discus with your right?"

The Discus Thrower had to admit this was a pretty good question. "Yes, that is true, I do throw with my right, but the left arm is equally important because it balances the weight and the thrust of my right arm. Without my left arm to counter what I do with my right, I would fall over."

Just as the Discus Thrower finished his explanation, he heard, for the second time in two days, the sound of approaching wheels squeaking on the floor. Soon, the lift truck with the large hook reappeared, stopping right in front of Peter Pan.

The Discus Thrower watched in amazement at what happened next: a few men tied a rope around Peter Pan and secured it to the big hook. He knew immediately that he was about to lose his roommate. He was stunned. It had barely been 24 hours. Nothing had ever happened this quickly to anything in the cage.

The Discus Thrower couldn't suppress his feelings of anger. Why was Peter Pan being rewarded with this attention? He was but a slacker who spent his time in Neverland, who believed, of all things, in fairies and dreamed of fantasy escapes with someone named Tinker Bell. He felt betrayed by his own values, by the discipline and hard work at the very core of his character, by the rigorous work ethic that had been responsible for his tremendous success as an athlete.

Is this my reward for having worked so hard? he wondered. He felt weak and disoriented. He continued to stare at Peter Pan, who now was suspended from the truck's hook as it slowly moved out of the cage. "Is this it?" whispered the Discus Thrower to himself. "Without even a goodbye?"

Everything was happening too quickly. Peter Pan was about to go out of sight, but just before the truck turned the corner, he swung very close to the Discus Thrower and for a brief moment they were face-to-face. The Discus Thrower gasped. Until then, he had only been able to see Peter Pan's back, but now, suddenly, he could see that Peter Pan was a handsome young man, completely different from what he had imagined.

The Discus Thrower's eyes darted quickly to the animals at Peter Pan's side, the deer and bunny and frog, each with adoring looks toward their master. And then once again he saw the horn stuffed with pink chewing gum. He felt lonely and jealous for the first time in his life, because Peter Pan had two things he craved desperately: freedom and companionship.

It was a sad moment for the once-proud athlete. Jealousy was not something he had ever experienced. It enveloped him. He didn't realize that Peter Pan was about to vanish around the corner. He had missed his chance to say goodbye.
Peter Pan, now swinging and turning as the truck maneuvered around the corner, felt dizzy. He wanted just once to see the Discus Thrower, the person he had shared this very strange experience with. He stretched as far as he could, and at last, he was able to turn just enough to see the great athlete who had stood behind him.

Peter Pan was awestruck. The Discus Thrower had huge, tense muscles in his legs and arm. *Wow*, he said to himself, *this guy's built. He is magnificent. He must be the strongest person in the world.* He had never seen anyone like him.

And then he noticed the Discus Thrower's serene and handsome face and strong profile. All of a sudden in that last second, just before the wall blocked their view of each other, their glances met. Peter Pan saw the Discus Thrower's eyes and felt their power and determination. *Oh, no*, Peter Pan thought, frantically, *he can't stay here any longer. He must get out.*

"Believe!" Peter Pan shouted to him, as he went swinging around the corner. "Start believing, Mr. Discus Thrower, and don't stop. Tinker Bell will rescue you!" And then it was quiet. The Discus Thrower was alone again.

8 • PETER PAN'S JOURNEY

The lift truck lumbered along, taking Peter Pan through dark corridors, out a huge door, across a parking lot, and then on a winding pathway toward the East River. Peter Pan saw a red powerboat tied up at the dock. Jeff was on it.

The next thing he knew, he was swinging over the stern of the boat and was lowered unceremoniously to the deck. Jeff took the rope, which was still knotted around him, and tied the loose end to the boat. Then the boat pulled out of the marina and headed down the river. It went past Peter

Pan's neighborhood at Carl Schurz Park. It looked so peaceful and familiar, he ached to be there. But the boat kept going, and in a few minutes the park had faded from view.

He had no idea where he was headed, but for the first time in a long time, he wasn't focused on himself. He was worried about the new friend he had left behind in the cage. Peter Pan was quick to admit that the guy had some very strange ideas: his rigorous work ethic, his sense of honor and concern for a place in history, and perhaps strangest of all, his faith in *something* that he felt would eventually lead him to freedom—and he didn't even believe in Tinker Bell.

When Peter Pan thought about how quickly he had escaped, he felt a bit guilty. But most of all, he was haunted by his last memory of the Discus Thrower, the sad eyes and the look of despair. Peter Pan regretted having to leave his new friend alone.

Despite all his odd notions, the Discus Thrower had made an impression on Peter Pan. As he watched the splashing waves, Peter Pan found himself thinking about the Olympic Games, the place called Athens, and the victories the Discus Thrower had achieved there.

47

Eventually, the boat pulled up to a pier, and Jeff helped the crew unload Peter Pan into a van not far away. Jeff got into the driver's seat and started the motor. A woman Peter Pan recognized from the morning visit got in too, and they drove away.

"Did you have time to examine the Discus Thrower?" she asked.

"Yes," Jeff said, "and it's not good news. The restoration will be difficult and expensive. He is missing an arm and the discus. We don't know what he originally looked like. We would need to hire an artist to create a rendering and use it to make the arm, hand, and discus molds. When I called the department with Peter Pan's restoration estimate, I mentioned the Discus Thrower project, and they said that they are trying to clear out old statuary which they don't have the funds to repair, and unfortunately the Discus Thrower is on that list. I think he is about to get turned into scrap metal."

"Oh, no," she said. "The Discus Thrower was in Central Park for many years and then in 1936 he was moved to Downing Stadium on Randall's Island for the U.S. Olympic Trials in which Jesse Owens competed. He is part of history. This is indeed terrible news."

Peter Pan, riding in the back of the van, heard every word and was frightened.

"I have an idea," Jeff said. "I know someone who might help us out. He loves art, and he was a discus thrower years ago. He won four Olympic gold medals in a row. I'll give him a call when I get to the foundry."

Peter Pan tried to think clearly. He was so scared he could hardly breathe. *Where is Tinker Bell?* he wondered. "We must do something now, or we may never see our new friend again."

Soon the van arrived at a big brick building. Peter Pan figured it was Jeff's foundry, but he didn't know what a foundry was. He was moved into a dark room and left alone with a lot to think about. He needed a plan.

9 • THE PLAN TO SAVE THE DISCUS THROWER

T ink?" he called out desperately as soon as he heard the door close and knew he was alone. "Tink, are you here? We've got a problem. We must get help for the Discus Thrower immediately." He was quite relieved when he heard the familiar sound she made, and then he saw her sparkle.

"You're interrupting me," Tinker Bell replied. "I've been checking this place out. It's an improvement over that other place, thankfully. So, what's the big problem?"

Peter Pan told her about the conversation he had heard in the van. He also told her they needed to get to Athens that very night. "If we can find the Discus Thrower's twin brother and get a photo of his arm, I think Jeff could use it as a guide to make a replacement. Maybe that would help lower the costs to restore him. Can you fly us there?"

"Who do you think you're talking to? Of course I can. I can fly anywhere," she said. Within seconds, they were out of the door and heading into darkening skies.

"Tink," Peter Pan said as they flew past the Brooklyn Bridge, "are you sure you know the way to Athens?"

"Of course I do. Second star to the right and straight on till morning. Just follow me, Peter Pan, and you will soon be in the ancient city of Athens, birthplace of democracy; the wonders of the Golden Age of Greece will be before you."

"What are you talking about?" he asked. "You sound like the Discus Thrower!"

"Well, I know a lot about this place. Wait until you see it!"

"Look," Tinker Bell said after they had flown a while in silence. "We've already made great progress. I can see Iceland."

"Really? How do you know it's Iceland? It's too dark to see anything," said Peter Pan.

"Fairies know these things; you'll have to trust me. It's a sixth sense. See those lights off in the distance? That's Reykjavik Airport. We're almost across the Atlantic Ocean."

"I hope you're right. I'm getting worried. Athens is a long way away according to the Discus Thrower. Why do you think you know how to get there?" Peter Pan was growing increasingly nervous about this venture, which had sounded so good just a few hours ago.

"And now, there's little Ireland," Tinker Bell remarked with special delight, ignoring him. She had great confidence in what she was doing and no interest in his anxiety. She had never known him to be anxious and found it strange.

"Oh sure, and how do you know that's Ireland?"

"Simple, it's the Emerald Isle. It even smells green. Can't you smell it?" But before Peter Pan had a chance to take a deep breath and determine if he could in fact smell a color, Tinker Bell announced, "Look, there's London!"

"London? *My* London where the Darlings live? Number 14 Kensington Gardens? Can we fly there and see the house?" he asked excitedly.

"Sure, did you think I had forgotten the way?"

"Of course not," replied Peter Pan. Then all of a sudden, he had an idea. He remembered that Mr. Darling kept a collection of maps on his desk in the library. Maybe, if the house were dark and everyone asleep, they could fly in through the

kitchen window, like they always used to do, and borrow a map of Athens. "Maybe we can drop in and find a map," he told Tinker Bell.

"You think I need a map? You still don't trust me. We're already halfway there."

He followed Tinker Bell as she led the way through the narrow streets to the familiar house in the middle of the block.

"Look, the window is open. We can fly in," he said. "But be quiet. It's dark, and everyone's asleep; don't awaken anyone."

They flew into the house with its charming details and colorful walls and furniture. Peter Pan tiptoed into Mr. Darling's library.

The old rolltop desk was just where Peter Pan remembered. He found the drawer and opened it quietly. Tinker Bell was flying around not paying any attention to him.

He flipped through the stack of maps and at last found one depicting old statues and buildings that looked like they were falling apart. He grabbed it.

He had never learned how to read, but he noticed that the word on the top was *G R E E C E* and tried sounding out the letters. Maybe this map was of Greece? He wasn't sure, but he took it and closed the drawer, and found Tinker Bell. They flew out the same window they had entered. He glanced back once more, locking the image in his mind.

10 • LONDON—
PARIS—ROME

Tinker Bell noticed the map in Peter Pan's
hand, but she didn't let it bother her. It
was too much fun being a tour guide to
get distracted. "Look just below, we are passing
over Paris. See the Eiffel Tower? And look, there's
the Louvre!"

"What's the Louvre?"

"It's the most famous museum in the world! It has the best collection of Renaissance art."

Peter Pan looked down and saw the museum. It looked like a castle, and it was lit up like the airport in Iceland. It was magnificent. He asked Tinker Bell to fly around it again so he could get a better view.

"I thought we were in a hurry," she said.

"Well, we are. We must be back in New York by tomorrow morning before the foundry opens, but can't we just take one more look?"

She nodded. They swooped down very low for one more look and then headed east. The sky was beginning to get lighter, making it easier to see below them. A huge city was straight ahead.

"What's that?" asked Peter Pan.

"Rome. See the huge cathedral? That's the Vatican, where Michelangelo painted the ceiling of the Sistine Chapel. And here is the ancient amphitheater, the Colosseum, where gladiators used to fight!" Once again, they swooped down to get a better view. Statues and fountains, one grand building after another sprang up in front of them as they flew across the city.

"Wow," Peter Pan gasped. He had no idea museums and cities like this even existed!

"Look, do you see a building up there on the hill?" she asked, pointing off in the distance.

"I see a lot of columns," Peter Pan said.

"That's the Acropolis in Greece. The sky is getting lighter. We might just make it to the Parthenon in time to see the sunrise!"

11 • ATHENS— THE SEARCH FOR BROTHER

hey made it. Just as they touched down, the top of a huge bright orange ball rose up from the distant horizon, one tiny sliver at a time. It was morning in Athens, Greece. The sun, in all its glory, was rising on the ancient city as it had for thousands of years. And as it did, the mighty columns of the Parthenon emerged from the darkness and seemed to grow in front of their eyes.

Tinker Bell smiled with pride. "I did it! We got to Athens just as I promised," she announced with glee while flitting about the columns to imaginary applause.

But Peter Pan wasn't interested in watching her performance. He stood as if in a trance, as still as the columns, unaware of anything else except the incredible view right in front of him.

Then suddenly, he remembered his mission. "Tink," he said, "we have to be in New York at sunrise, and the sun is coming up now. We must find the Discus Thrower's brother this minute and get out of here."

"I never promised I would help you find him. I only agreed to get you here. Now, if you don't mind, there are a few things I would like to do . . . maybe get a little tan . . . and see if I can find a gorgeous Greek fairy somewhere."

"Come on, Tink, I need your help. The sun is already rising, and we must be back in New York by the time Jeff comes to work."

"You silly. We have lots of time. The sun doesn't rise in New York for another six hours."

"Really?" he said, giving the notion some thought. "OK, I guess that makes sense since we are here now and there is only one sun and it's a long way from New York. So we've got six hours before we need to be back?"

"Right, boss," she said. They sat in silence for a few more moments. He had never seen anything like this. As the seconds ticked away, the ancient stones all around them came alive and soon the entire Acropolis was bathed in golden morning light.

"Time is up, Tinker Bell, we have to start now to find Brother."

"Well, all right. Do you have any idea where he might be? I think this is a pretty big city, and it looks like there are statues everywhere!"

He reached into his pocket. "Trust me, you are in good hands. I just happen to have a map," he said with some pride.

"But," said Tinker Bell, "you just so happen to not know how to read."

"You have a good point. But, according to the lecture I had to listen to last night from the Discus Thrower, Brother is at a stadium located in the Zappeion Gardens. Maybe there is a picture of him on this map." Peter Pan opened the map and spread it on the step he was sitting on. There was a huge photo on the cover, and he recognized the Parthenon. And in the same photo, just to the west of the Parthenon, he saw a stadium surrounded by gardens.

"I'll bet this is the Zappeion Gardens," he said with his finger on the spot.

"Look over there," said Tinker Bell.

Off in the distance, toward the city, she could see a stadium! They set off immediately. As they flew closer to the stadium, they saw just what they were looking for. The statue of Brother was standing in the middle of a garden, and behind him was the entrance to a beautiful white marble stadium. The statue looked exactly like the Discus Thrower, with the same intense stare and strong body.

"Wow," said Peter Pan, "look at him: he has both arms, and they are over his head with the discus between his fingertips, just like our friend told us." Now Peter Pan knew what the Discus Thrower had been trying to tell him about the importance of his left arm! They walked closer to the statue.

In this beautiful city amidst the splendor of the gardens, surrounded by statues all shimmering in the golden sunrise, Brother seemed like a different statue than the Discus Thrower who was at this moment locked in a cage. Brother was magnificent! Peter Pan tried to think of how to introduce himself to Brother. He wasn't sure what to say. He looked around and was relieved to discover that they were alone. He was glad it was so early in the morning. Only the birds were awake, busy looking for breadcrumbs.

12 • The Conversation with Brother

G ood morning, Mr. Discus Thrower," said Peter Pan, mustering up a degree of politeness he didn't know he had. There was silence. "Good morning to you," he said again, getting a little closer. Peter Pan waited for what seemed to be a very long time.

He was nervous. He wasn't used to being ignored and wondered if, somehow, he had become invisible, like Tinker Bell is sometimes. Maybe Brother hadn't heard him or couldn't see him? At last, the silence was broken.

"Oh, good morning, I didn't know anyone was here," Brother said in a voice just like the Discus Thrower's. Peter Pan was shocked at the similarity. "You are up bright and early today," Brother continued. "Usually no one comes until 9 o'clock when the buses arrive."

"Well, we didn't need a bus; we just flew here. We're from New York."

"Really? That's a long way away. I once knew someone who went there, but that was years ago. I haven't heard from him since he left."

Peter Pan paused for a minute. "I think I know who you are talking about, sir," he stammered. "Is it your brother?"

"Yes, how did you know?"

"I was with him yesterday, and he needs help. He has lost his left arm and discus, and he has been kept in a storage cage and hasn't seen daylight for at least 25 years. If I don't find a drawing or photo

of his arm very soon, as a guide toward his restoration, I am afraid he will be sold to a junkyard."
There! The sad message was out, and then there
was more silence, which was finally broken by the
familiar voice.

"My brother? You know him?" he asked, looking
off into the distance. "I never thought I would
hear of him again after all these years. I am so
glad you came. I will do anything I can to help
him. Tell me again, what do you need?"

"It's about his arm. Since you two are twins,
I thought that if I could find a photo of you, particularly your left arm, to bring back to New York,
it would help the bronze foundry re-create his
missing arm and discus. I am afraid that without
a photo of what he looked like, we will not be able
to save him."

"Actually, I think his arm might have been larger
than mine. He was always better than I was at the
discus. But," Brother said after a few seconds,
"I might have a solution. There is a photo of me
on a postcard."

"He told me all about how you both were discus
throwers. I think the postcard might work."
This was a very clever solution, Peter Pan thought.

"OK. I think I know how you can get one. At 8 o'clock, in just a few minutes, Dimitriades, who runs the store over there," Brother said, nodding to a little building at the left of the terrace, "unlocks the door, goes inside, and gets a broom and sweeps the steps and the area around his shop. He has done this every morning for many years. When you see him, tell him what you need. He is a kind man; we have been friends for a long time, and I know he will help us."

"Great idea," said Peter Pan.

"Good. And now since we have a few minutes, I would like to tell you how glad I am that you came. My brother and I were close when we were younger. We grew up together. But he was much more competent than I was, and in this respect, we were very different. He wanted to excel in everything he did. He practiced tirelessly and worked very hard. He wanted to be the best discus thrower ever! But it is a very complicated sport, and I just wasn't as good."

"What is so difficult about it?" Peter Pan decided he would try to understand this sport now, and besides, he had a few moments to hang out before the store opened. Brother seemed pleased with the question and happy to talk.

"Unlike the shot put, discus throwing is not only about using all your strength to throw. The discus is actually cradled in the palm of the hand. It touches only the fingertips and is propelled by the faintest, most subtle motion. The act of throwing a discus combines strength with finesse. The thrower must of course have a very large hand, but even then, many throwers are ineffective because they lack the instinctive ability to cradle the discus using very little pressure but just enough to keep it secure while spinning faster and faster."

He continued. "A good thrower must also have tremendous balance. My brother had mastered this, and he dominated the sport in Greece. When the opportunity to travel to America came along, he never hesitated. He accepted immediately. I'm not sure he ever thought about the fact that he would be leaving his home and family behind and that perhaps we would never see each other again."

"Could you have gone, too?"

"Yes. He invited me to join him. It was a very difficult decision to make, and eventually it led to our separation because I decided to stay here in my home, Athens. Soon after he left, I stopped competing all together. Without his company, it just wasn't the same. Now, after all these years, I still miss him very much.

"I am here at the most beautiful park in the world, the grand entrance to the site of the modern Olympic Games, the place where the 2004 marathon ended. I know how lucky I am.

"But every day, when I see families, young brothers and sisters together enjoying themselves, my thoughts drift back many years, and I picture us together as children, and I am sad."

"I am sorry," said Peter Pan. "I never had a brother or sister, but I think I can understand how difficult it must be to be separated. And I am sorry to have brought you such sad news."

"I always imagined that he went on to even bigger and better things in America," said Brother. "In Greece, Olympians are treated with great respect. How could this happen to my brother, such an honorable and talented athlete? Living in a storage cage for 25 years? I am so sorry and so sad. Thank you for trying to help him."

13 • FINDING THE POSTCARD

Brother stopped talking for a moment, and then after a pause, he said, "Quick, Dimitriades just arrived—hurry, the postcards are on the left just inside the door!" Tinker Bell, who had been waiting patiently while Peter Pan and Brother talked, jumped up and flew toward the store. Peter Pan ran to follow her. Sure enough, Dimitriades came out of the store, broom in hand.

"Hello," said Peter Pan. "I was just talking to your friend the Discus Thrower, and we wonder if you can help us?"

Dimitriades came closer and spoke. "Of course, young man, he is a very good friend. What can I do for you?"

Peter Pan explained as best he could about Brother's twin in New York and the need for a postcard. "You don't have to say another word," Dimitriades said. "Let me get you a postcard, and I wish you lots of luck with what you are trying to do. You are a good lad."

And with that, he handed Peter Pan a card with a photo of Brother on it. He waved a quick goodbye and started sweeping.

"Mission accomplished," Peter Pan told Brother, seconds later. "And now we're out of here. If we fly very quickly and don't get distracted, we might have time to stop and see your brother on our way back to the foundry."

"Oh, please do, and please tell him how much I miss him." Brother thought for a moment and then added, "You have done so much already, but there is something I must ask of you. Could you come back one day and let me know how he is?"

"I think we can do that," replied Peter Pan after getting a nod from Tinker Bell. "It was really a breeze getting here!"

"Goodbye for now," Brother said. "I will think of you and await your return. Have a good trip." Peter Pan and Tinker Bell waved and set off. They flew in silence for quite a while, thinking about the new friend they were leaving behind and reflecting on the gravity of the situation. They *must* save the Discus Thrower.

14 • FLYING WEST, AHEAD OF THE SUN

The trip west, back to New York, was different from the trip east. There were no stops for sightseeing. Peter Pan and Tinker Bell had only one thing on their mind, and that was to get back home fast.

They flew straight through, ahead of the rising sun, preoccupied with the commitment they had made to save the Discus Thrower. Now that they had met Brother, both he and the Discus Thrower seemed like part of the family, and the burden of their pledge to help felt like a heavy weight. They barely spoke as they flew side by side.

It was dusk all the way back. Europe was mostly a blur, and the Atlantic Ocean was just a huge dark expanse broken by an occasional whitecap on the tip of a wave glimmering in the moonlight.

The rising orange sun was just beginning to reflect off the windowed skyline of the giant New York City skyscrapers when Peter Pan and Tinker Bell approached the corridor of buildings that stretched along the East River. Randall's Island was in full view in front of them.

"Do we have time to stop and see him?" Tinker Bell asked.

"We have to," Peter Pan replied. "We have to tell him about Brother, but we must be quick."

Randall's Island was already bursting with activity. Trucks and cars and golf carts were going in all directions. Buses unloaded passengers wearing warm-up suits and carrying tennis rackets or baseball bats.

"Such activity," whispered Peter Pan. They flew through the familiar door of the storage building and made their way very quickly to the Discus Thrower. He was just as they had left him; he hadn't moved an inch. It was sad to see him now, still amidst the clutter, covered with dust, in such sharp contrast to the twin they had left just a while ago in the Athenian sun.

Peter Pan broke the silence with a quiet "Hi."

"Is that you, Peter Pan, my friend?" the Discus Thrower asked.

"Yes, I'm here with Tinker Bell, but we are in a hurry to get back to the foundry before they open, and we can't stay long. We wanted to tell you that we made it to Athens, and we saw your brother this morning. He is well, and he asked us to tell you how much he misses you." Peter Pan thought he heard the Discus Thrower sigh, but he wasn't sure.

"We got what we needed," added Tinker Bell. "We have a photograph of your brother, and we think Jeff can use it as a guide to re-create your arm."

"I don't know what to say," said the Discus Thrower. "I am overwhelmed. A message from my long-lost brother and the possibility that I might get my arm back . . ."

They were about to fly off when Peter Pan remembered he had a question for the Discus Thrower. It was something he very much wanted to know. "There is something you could help me with, Mr. Discus Thrower," he said. "Do you know what a *foundry* is? That's where I am going now."

"Sure. A foundry is a workshop for casting metal. I had a friend when I was a child in Greece whose father worked in a foundry. We would often visit and watch his dad work, making metal into liquid and then casting it into an object. I found it quite fascinating."

"Thank you, I was very curious." He realized that he had been a little embarrassed about having to admit he didn't know what the word meant, but the Discus Thrower was very kind and didn't make him feel badly.

"It is good to be able to help you after all you have done for me! I hardly know what to say."

"We're friends," said Peter Pan. "You don't need to say anything. This is what friends do for each other. Now we must go, but Tinker Bell will come back later today to let you know if there is any news. I am going to be getting repaired now, at the foundry," he said with a smile at using this new word, "and I will be there for a while."

"I'll be right here," the Discus Thrower said with a bit of humor, and off they flew.

15 • Jeff Finds the Postcard

It was 8:25 a.m. when Peter Pan and Tinker Bell quietly snuck back into the foundry with just enough time to leave the postcard on the work desk in the casting room. Just minutes later, the door opened, and Peter Pan heard Jeff's voice as he approached, turning the lights on along the way. Jeff noticed the postcard immediately and called Eddie to come and take a look.

"Wow," he said. "The Discus Thrower seems to have a twin in Greece. Look at this. I wonder how this card got here."

"It's a great photo," Eddie said. "Now we know what his arm looked like. We could use this as a model for the restoration."

Then he took the card from Jeff and studied it closer. "There's only one problem: the angle of this photo doesn't show how the fingers hold the discus."

Jeff agreed that this was a problem and paused for a moment. Then he had an idea. "Al Oerter," he said. "I called him yesterday and asked him if he would be interested in going to see the Discus Thrower statue later today. He said he would. He will know the correct position for the hand."

"That's a great idea," agreed Eddie. "He's a good guy. He once competed on Randall's Island."

"Yes, we're lucky," said Jeff. "Let's start working on our friend Peter Pan until he gets here." He looked at his notes. "Let's see, the patina has eroded, we've got a scraped knee and a scratched deer's nose, and the tip of his feather needs repair, as well as a few dents. Let's see how fast we can turn him around. They want him back soon."

Who's Al Oerter? wondered Peter Pan. "Ever heard of him, Tinker Bell?" But there was no answer. She was sound asleep. A team of workers arrived and began to crawl all over Peter Pan, rubbing out scrapes and smoothing out nicks, mixing samples of patina, working on the base. Peter Pan was trying to be patient, but it was difficult with all the pulling and pushing. At last it was lunchtime, and everyone left him alone. Then, in the silence, he heard a new voice. Someone had just arrived, and everyone sounded very excited to see him. "Who on earth is this?" he said aloud.

16 • A Third Discus Thrower?

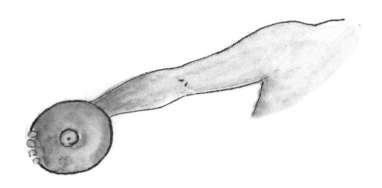

Peter Pan couldn't believe what he was hearing. The person who had just arrived was being introduced as another discus thrower! If he was hearing correctly, Jeff had said that his name was Al Oerter and he had won four Olympic gold medals in discus throwing.

All this commotion awakened Tinker Bell. "What?" she gasped. "Now there are three discus throwers? I think things are getting a little out of hand! There's our friend the Discus Thrower, there's Brother in Athens, and now there's a guy named Al Oerter who is a discus thrower too? The place is loaded with them. Life was much easier when we were at Carl Schurz Park. I want to go back there now."

"*Shhhh*, let's listen to what he's saying," said Peter Pan.

Al was speaking. "I'm so glad you called me. I'm in town just for a few days visiting friends in Astoria. It's perfect timing."

Al looked at the postcard, and after a few seconds he said, "I remember the statue from the days when I competed at Downing Stadium. I always thought he brought me luck. So, he has a twin in Athens? I never knew that. Yes, we must restore the statue. What can I do to help?"

"Let's go to Randall's Island to see him," said Jeff. Tinker Bell hopped into the car with them and tried to listen to their conversation. She wanted to be able to tell Peter Pan what they talked about.

Jeff told Al of his concerns about restoring the Discus Thrower, that they needed to know how the arm and discus would have been designed, that he had found the postcard on his desk with a photo of a twin statue in Athens. When they got to Randall's Island, they walked into the storage building and then into the Discus Thrower's cage.

"Wow," said Al. "He looks terrible!"

Jeff explained to Al how the photo showed the design of the arm but not how the fingers held the discus.

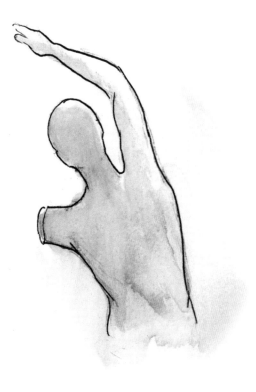

"I think I can help," said Al. "The statue uses an ancient throwing technique which evolved over the years, and in 1900 competitors changed to a style where the whole body rotates around. The statue's motion was of a different sort. It started with both arms overhead. The arms were swung down and back up. Eventually the discus was released." Al demonstrated how this would have been done, how the fingers would have balanced the discus, and he offered to advise Jeff during the restoration project.

When Tinker Bell got back, she told Peter Pan the good news, that Al could advise Jeff about the

holding of the discus. Then she told Peter Pan how kind and handsome this latest discus thrower was. "Maybe all discus throwers are gorgeous," she said.

Peter Pan had never felt jealous—he was very content with his life in Neverland—but he did feel a little bit of concern, and then he shrugged it off. He had too many things to focus on without being envious of three discus throwers, and besides, he was very glad that Al Oerter had arrived!

Tinker Bell also told Peter Pan about the conversation Jeff and Al had on the trip back to the foundry. Al asked Jeff how the repair would be done and how much it would cost. Something about a process called "lost wax ceramic shell" with clay molds, then wax molds, then bronze casting.

"It made no sense," she said, "and I can't imagine what they were talking about, but Al nodded like he understood."

Then she told Peter Pan that after discussing the process, Jeff and Al talked about how they might get the funds to pay for the work.

"Al is determined to figure out a way, and he has a great idea," Tinker Bell said. "He mentioned a man named Bloom-something who likes art and is a philanthropist. He said he would speak to him about the project." Remembering all these complicated big words made Tinker Bell tired, and she started to yawn. But she continued. "Al said that restoring the statue meant a lot to him not only because it involved his treasured sport, but because it involved art. He said that he had begun to paint. Maybe that's why he wants to help so much."

She yawned again and was about to fall asleep when she remembered one more thing. "When we walked into the cage, the Discus Thrower whispered to me that he recognized Al and remembered seeing him years ago at competitions at Randall's Island. I think our buddy Al is for real," Tinker Bell said. And then finally she lay down and fell asleep.

Peter Pan was curious and wanted to keep talking, but Tinker Bell was snoring. He was overjoyed with all her news. This could be the lucky break Peter Pan had been hoping for and the Discus Thrower desperately needed. He began to relax for the first time in a long time. He was not used to stress and didn't like feeling worried or concerned.

Then he started to think about himself, which oddly he hadn't done for a long time. He realized that Tinker Bell hadn't commented about his appearance, about how much better he was beginning to look now that his feather and scrapes were fixed. His feelings were a little hurt, he had to admit.

But then, in just a few minutes, the workers came back and there was more pulling and tugging, and he was once again preoccupied. It was all he could do to control himself and not complain, but after all, he remembered, they were only trying to help him. So, he closed his eyes and pretended he was back at Carl Schurz Park and that it was a beautiful sunny day, and then he allowed himself to imagine that perhaps, one day soon, the Discus Thrower would be just across the river at Randall's Island enjoying a sunny day outside as well.

17 • PETER PAN GOES HOME

The next morning, Peter Pan slept late. He was exhausted from all the shining and polishing that had gone on the day before, after his scrapes and wounds were fixed. Tinker Bell was exhausted too and sound asleep when Jeff came in, flipped the lights on, and started to give directions to the team. "Eddie," Jeff said, "get the padding blankets and wrap him up really good."

Peter Pan soon was smothered in warm blankets, secured in place by several large ropes. Then he was lifted onto a rolling rack and rolled out to the same van that had brought him there a few days before. "Tinker Bell, are you here?" he called out softly when he heard the motor start.

"Yes," she whispered. "What's happening now?"

"I think we're going home!" he said.

A few minutes later he was loaded into the boat, the same boat that had taken him from Randall's Island. The motor started, and now he knew he was going home. Before long, the boat slowed down and turned, and then it bumped a little against what he thought was a dock. He was lifted off the boat, and a few minutes later he was set down on his familiar rock. The ropes were untied, the blankets fell away, and suddenly he heard cheers and applause and saw lots of children with balloons and grown-ups who were all applauding and shouting, "Welcome home, Peter Pan!"

He looked at the crowd, and he saw Al and Jeff and a few other familiar people. Finally, the crowd began to leave. A few photographers stayed to take photos, and then they left as well. But Peter

Pan was glad to see that Al was still there. He had grown fond of him.

Al was talking to a man who had been standing with him. They seemed to be discussing something very seriously. Peter Pan struggled to hear what they were saying.

"Mike, I'm really glad to see you," said Al.

"You too, Al," said Mike. "I heard there is something you want to talk about." Peter Pan wondered who Mike was.

"Yes, there is," Al said. "You may not remember, but years ago there was a beautiful bronze statue called the Discus Thrower at the entrance to Downing Stadium. It was placed there for the grand opening of the stadium in 1936, the year Jesse Owens competed in the Olympic Trials there. I remember it being there when I competed, and I always touched it thinking it would bring me luck."

"And it usually did," said Mike with a chuckle, thinking of Al's four Olympic gold medals.

"Yes, that's true. I was very fortunate" Al agreed. "But it's really terrible what happened to the statue. Several years later, its arm and discus were taken, and it was removed from its pedestal. It has been in storage ever since, for about 25 years. Jeff looked at the statue a few days ago and has a restoration plan. He is ready to go, but we are still searching for funding. Can you help? If we get your support now, Jeff can go over to Randall's Island on the boat and pick up the Discus Thrower."

"I would be delighted to help with this project," Mike replied. "You know how much I enjoy supporting the arts for our city and how much I admire you, Al. I could never turn this opportunity down."

"Oh my gosh," whispered Tinker Bell. "He's going to do it!"

Peter Pan was trying hard to control himself, he was so happy. The men said goodbye. Jeff, after hearing this good news, got back on the boat and headed to Randall's Island.

"Go with him, Tinker Bell," Peter Pan said. "Go tell the Discus Thrower what's happening!"

18 • THE DISCUS THROWER SEES SUNSHINE

"I believe...I believe!"

T inker Bell got to the storage cage ahead of Jeff and had just a few minutes to tell the Discus Thrower the good news, that a donor had been found and his restoration was to begin.

Clank—the lights went on, interrupting Tinker Bell in the middle of her story. As the familiar sound of Tom and Scott's voices and footsteps drew closer, the Discus Thrower tried to process what Tinker

Bell had just told him, that he was about to get out of the cage, at last.

After all these years the moment he had been waiting for was approaching, and it all seemed to be happening so very quickly. Scott unlocked the padlock and swung the cage doors open. They began to rearrange his fellow companions in the cage to make room for the Discus Thrower's exit. The World War I Infantry Fighter was pushed farther back, and the pair of eagles on the other side were eased closer together. The Victorian lampposts were moved to another part of the cage.

Then he saw Jeff and heard the approaching sound of wheels squeaking on the floor. Soon, the lift truck with its large hook appeared, the same one that had taken Peter Pan. This time, it stopped right in front of the Discus Thrower, and he watched as the same routine played out again, but this time for him! A rope was tied around the Discus Thrower and secured to the big hook on the lift truck. He was hoisted up off the ground, and slowly the truck pulled away and moved him out of the cage, swinging slightly.

The moment had come! He really was leaving, creeping very slowly down the long corridor, out the big garage doors, and at long last into the afternoon sunshine. The warmth of the sun felt so good on his dry and dirty body, and the light cool breeze, smelling just a little salty, seemed very familiar. It was exactly as he remembered it some 25 years ago when he last stood at the entrance to the stadium.

He was wrapped in blankets, hoisted onto a boat, and secured very tightly to its stern. The boat engine started. Jeff climbed aboard and said goodbye to Scott and Tom.

The boat headed south down the East River, past the Randall's Island ball fields and the teams of kids playing soccer and baseball.

The Discus Thrower looked west toward Manhattan and was awestruck by the massive skyscrapers lining the river. Gentle waves rocked the boat a bit as he breathed in the salty cool air. He thought he must be dreaming when suddenly he heard someone calling him.

"Mr. Discus Thrower," said a familiar voice. It was Peter Pan. He was waving to the Discus Thrower from a garden near the water's edge, surrounded by the most beautiful flowers. He gleamed in the sunlight.

"I believe," the Discus Thrower called back. "I believe," he said again. Then the boat took a turn down the river and disappeared from view. Peter Pan remembered that he had told the Discus Thrower to do just that, to believe, when he left him a few days ago in the cage.

19 • The Discus Thrower at the Foundry

The Discus Thrower arrived at the foundry feeling more and more alive with every new minute, and the feeling continued for the weeks he spent there. He was overjoyed to be out of the cage and was fascinated with all the activity around him.

After the boat arrived at the foundry dock, he was transported into the foundry and set on a base on the floor. A team of workers assembled, and he listened attentively as Jeff described the restoration plan for re-creating his arm, hand, and discus. An artist sat next to him, and he watched intently as she sketched an image of what would become his future arm and hand and discus, often referring to the photo postcard of Brother in Athens.

Jeff said that if they had something he called a "negative mold" of the arm it would have helped, and the Discus Thrower wished Tinker Bell could go back and get it. Without this mold, Jeff said, they would need to fabricate a new one using the three-dimensional drawing the artist was making to guide them.

At the same time, the place where his arm had been severed was studied and measured over and over. The replacement must fit perfectly with the remaining part of his arm. The design of the fingers holding the discus was another issue that had been discussed with Al. Photographs had been taken of Al cradling the discus in his hand, which the artist now referred to in drawing the future hand and discus.

Soon a clay mold of his arm was ready to be fitted to his upper arm. This was a wonderful moment for the Discus Thrower. It wasn't his permanent arm, but with this temporary mold in place, the

Discus Thrower had the sense of a complete body. It would take more time to make his real arm out of bronze, but it felt good just to have something there where his real arm had once been.

One day, a group of visitors arrived. He could tell this would be a special day, because that morning all work had stopped. The floor was cleaned, tools that had been tossed around were carefully stored, coffee cups were put away. He heard Jeff say that the New York City Art Commission was coming to look at the remodeling. When the commission of about 10 people arrived, they gathered around the Discus Thrower, looked at the temporary arm, hand, and discus, and talked about size and angles and placement.

They also discussed treatment of the Discus Thrower's joints, which had begun to separate, and the surface corrosion and pitting that were due to his general lack of care for so many years. Correcting this would require extensive work. Once again, he was reminded how lucky he was to be getting the help he so badly needed.

20 • THE NEW ARM IS MADE

ventually, the Art Commission finished its review, gave approval, and left. The foundry team stayed and celebrated. Now they had the go-ahead to cast the bronze pieces. At the same time, Jeff said, the welders could start repairing the Discus Thrower's joints and the surface areas that had been damaged over the years.

"The first step in making the bronze arm, hand, and discus," he said, "is to remove the clay replicas, which we'll use in casting the wax molds."

The Discus Thrower knew this meant he would be parting with his temporary arm, but he understood that eventually he would get his permanent arm back. So he relaxed and watched as the team removed his clay arm. Then he saw them put a two-piece plaster shell around the clay arm, one piece on the top and one on the bottom. This was all very strange to the Discus Thrower, but he was always interested in learning, and so he listened and watched as everyone around him worked. He knew that they were skilled craftsmen. He was confident that ultimately all would be OK.

Next, after the two pieces of plaster shell had been allowed to set and harden, the team very carefully separated them from the clay replica inside. They took the two pieces of the plaster shell and put them back together, securing them with bands of metal. Then they proceeded to fill them with melted wax through a hole at the top, to reproduce the arm as a wax mold.

This is a lot of work, the Discus Thrower said to himself. *It is no wonder that it took so long to get approval.* The crew let the wax dry while they ate lunch. After lunch, they very slowly and carefully broke off the plaster, revealing his new arm, hand, and discus in wax.

The next step he found fascinating. They took the wax replica and dipped it into some kind of white goo in a big tub. The goo hardened and became a fireproof shell around the wax replica, and they let it dry. Then, on the top of the shell, they put two spouts, and on the bottom, they put what looked like a drain. Now he was thoroughly intrigued. In a furnace in the corner of the room, they heated several bricks of solid bronze, which Jeff called "ingots," until they were a bright red liquid.

The thermometer registered 2,000 degrees. *Wow, that's hot*, he thought.

They put the white goo shell with the wax replica still inside into a very hot oven, which they called a "kiln." Using long clamps, they held the shell upright so that the melted wax could drain out the bottom. Then they put a plug into that drain. Next, they poured the melted bronze into one of the spouts at the top.

Jeff watched intently and said, "It's full," when he could see that the bronze had worked its way up to the second spout. Now the entire inside of the shell was filled with liquid bronze.

Everyone took a break. They had been working hard, and it was very hot in the room. When they came back, they started chipping away very carefully at the plaster shell. His new bronze arm, hand, and discus started to emerge from the plaster. When they were finished, they laid the bronze creations on the worktable and admired their work. Everyone was exhausted. Slowly they put their coats on, turned off the lights, and left the foundry. It was dark. The Discus Thrower was exhausted, too. It had been an amazing day!

21 • WELDING STARTS

The Discus Thrower was so excited, it was very difficult for him to sleep. Finally, morning arrived, and he knew that today he would get his new arm! He heard the work crew arrive and wondered what would happen next. Then he heard Jeff tell his team that this morning they would weld his arm in place and then get to the "chasing stage" in the afternoon. He didn't know what that meant.

Welding torches were lit to prime the edge of the new arm, and then it was pressed onto the remaining stub of his old arm. The crew carefully held the two ends in place until they were permanently attached. He was complete, just like he had been many years ago. What a feeling! But the process was not over.

Next was the chasing stage, which consisted of filing, finishing, and cleaning. First, the joining seam on his arm was smoothed over so that there was no difference between the upper arm, which was original, and the lower arm, which was brand-new.

Then all the bumps and marks on his surface and his other joints, which welders had been working on, were smoothed over. His legs, feet, head, right arm, back, and front all were filed and buffed. Lunchtime came, and they stopped working.

Maybe they are done? he wondered.

But after lunch, the team came back again to apply what he heard them call "patina," a mixture of acid and water that was brushed all over him and then heated using a torch. The patina made him a beautiful dark ebony color.

Then the final step in his recovery began. He was rubbed all over with a creamy wax, and this really felt good. When the waxing was done, the team stopped to admire him, the way people did years ago when they saw him. He realized, as he looked down at his body, that he actually radiated in the foundry lights.

Soon the foundry was quiet, and he felt a sense of peace settle in as the team slowly turned off the lights and closed the door, leaving him for the night. But he knew he was not alone. He heard a sound and then realized it was Tinker Bell.

"You look awesome," she said. "And handsome too!"

"Hi," he replied. "How are you and Peter Pan?"

"We are so excited," she said. "You are going home tomorrow! I just heard Jeff tell Eddie to get the boat ready for the trip back to Randall's Island in the morning. He said that there will be a big welcome back celebration for you."

"Wow," the Discus Thrower said, "I am so happy to be going back to my park!"

"And tonight," said Tinker Bell, "I am flying to Athens to tell Brother the good news. I need to leave now so I will be back in the morning to watch you sail past Peter Pan at Carl Schurz Park."

"I am so grateful to you and Peter Pan," he said. "Please tell my brother I miss him and thank him for the postcard. And tell him how wonderful it is that now we are both where we want to be."

She said she would, and then she was off into the night. The Discus Thrower watched Tinker Bell fly away, and then he was alone in the foundry for one last night, alone with his new self. He had never been happier. He enjoyed the peace and quiet and having time to reflect on his experience at the foundry and the remaking of his arm. Peter Pan was right.

My good fortune was not due to my hard work, training, and discipline, but to the support and generosity of others, he thought to himself.

Tomorrow he would be going home, and tomorrow night he would be outside under the stars. Slowly, he drifted off to sleep, very contentedly.

22 • THE DISCUS THROWER GOES HOME

Abeam of sun awakened him early the next morning. It was July, one of his favorite months. The sun rose early and set late, so the days were long and bright and warm. The Summer Olympics were held in July. And back when he was competing, he would wake up early to practice and prepare for the next event.

Later, when he came to New York City, his summer mornings were filled with activity in the park: kids, families, and adults arriving for games, celebrating the warm summer days.

Suddenly he was jolted back to reality by the voices of the crew as they arrived, much earlier than usual. This was a different day, and the Discus Thrower knew it. Unlike other mornings, no one picked up tools or put on work jackets. Eddie came in with several large pads and wrapped them around him. Jeff tied them in place with rope. Then, a lift truck arrived, and once again he was lifted off his base and moved out of the building and onto the boat and secured. The motor started, and slowly the boat pulled away.

It was a glorious morning. Full sun, blue sky, warm breezes, and just a little motion of the boat in the waves. He felt the warmth of the sun. He could see other boats on the river, tugboats pushing barges, ferryboats filled with passengers, the Circle Line crowded with sightseers who waved to him, sleek sailboats, and powerful yachts. He watched the traffic on FDR Drive: yellow taxis and cars of all colors and motorcycles, too. It was all so new to him, and he just loved seeing the city come alive for another day.

The boat turned a bit at a bend in the river, and then he remembered Peter Pan. He thought the area looked familiar from his trip several weeks ago to the foundry. He searched the landscape for his friend, and just then, he heard him calling.

"Good morning, Mr. Discus Thrower," Peter Pan said.

"Hi, Peter Pan. I am going home," replied the Discus Thrower.

"The city is having a big party today to celebrate your homecoming," Peter Pan told him.

"Thank you! I am so grateful to you and Tinker Bell," he said, and then they were out of sight of each other.

The boat slowed a bit and headed toward the familiar dock at Randall's Island. He felt the bump as it gently nudged the edge of the dock, saw Jeff jump off, and then watched as a lift truck arrived.

I am home, he thought. He was used to the routine and knew what was going to happen. Eddie untied the ropes and secured him to the huge hook that lifted him up out of the boat. The truck started moving, and he could see the storage building in the distance. It frightened him a little to see it, but the truck headed off in a different direction, and he never saw it again.

Slowly, the truck moved along the pathway, gently swinging the Discus Thrower with the motion. It stopped in front of a beautiful pink marble base, the one he had stood on until he was removed from it that bitter cold day many years ago.

Large bronze letters on the side of the base read "THE DISCUS THROWER." It was four feet high, and he remembered that when he stood on it, he could see above the crowd and easily watch the activity on the fields. He had forgotten how magnificent it was. Now he was full of joy in anticipation of standing on it again.

The belt around his waist and chest held him securely as he was raised up higher until he was right over the base. Then he was lowered down and safely locked into place. Everything stopped for a moment. It was silent. At last, there he was, back where he had once been. His long journey was finally over!

23 • THE WELCOME HOME PARTY

Moments later, Tom and Scott arrived holding a huge gold-colored cloth. They stopped for a moment and admired him, and then they unfolded the cloth and covered him with it from head to toe. *Oh no!* Had he gone through this journey only to spend his life under a gold cloth?

Then he noticed a tiny hole in the cloth. If he squinted, he could look through it and see what was going on. Lots of people and kids were walking toward him, sitting down around him. He could see Tom and Scott tying ropes along the bottom of the gold cloth. And then he saw Al, and Al's friend Mike.

Finally, everyone was quiet, and Al and Mike spoke to the crowd about this special day of celebration because the Discus Thrower was back home. Everyone cheered. They asked the kids to hold on to the ends of the ropes, which were attached to what they called a "gold shroud." He assumed they were talking about the gold cloth.

Then they started counting down: "Ten, Nine, Eight, Seven, Six, Five, Four, Three, Two, One, PULL!" When the ropes were pulled, the shroud fell away, and there he was. Everyone applauded. The children had blue Frisbees, which they tossed into the air in celebration.

The Discus Thrower wasn't used to being the center of attention like he had been many years ago, and he felt a little bit awkward. But the applause as the gold shroud was pulled away, the smiles on everyone's faces, and the children who came closer and gently patted him were a beautiful welcome home. Eventually the crowd dispersed, and everyone went back to their games and activities. He saw Al and Mike shake hands and walk away, and he was left in peace.

The sun began to set. The huge orange ball moved slowly down toward the spectacular buildings of the New York City skyline, and finally it disappeared behind them.

A peaceful hush settled around him, birds stopped flying about, kids and adults left the park, the air was a little cooler, and he looked around and marveled at the beauty of his surroundings. Night began to fall, and he took a deep breath of wonderful, salty air.

24 • MESSAGE FROM BROTHER

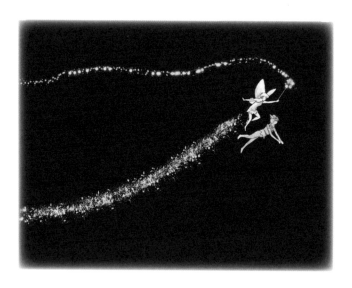

S uddenly he heard something very familiar. Peter Pan was heading toward him, with Tinker Bell at his side.

"It is so good to see you here," said Peter Pan. "You look fabulous with your new arm and discus. Welcome home!"

"Thank you! I am so glad to see you both," the Discus Thrower said.

"We have a message for you from Brother," said Tinker Bell. "I saw him last night. He is so happy that you are home. He had an idea. If you look up at the stars tonight at 9 o'clock, he will do the same thing in Athens. It will be 4 in the morning for him. You both will be looking at the sky at the same time, and he will be thinking of you."

"That's a great idea," said the Discus Thrower.

"He said that if you do this every night at the same time, he will too, and you will have this time together," said Tinker Bell.

"It is almost 9," Peter Pan said, "and we don't want you to be late for Brother. We'll be leaving soon. But first, I want to thank you, Mr. Discus Thrower, for all I learned from you. You taught me about history, about the Olympics, and about Greece, and about growing up and the importance of having goals, and training and practicing and having faith in the future. I am actually trying to learn how to read. I must admit that the first time I met you I thought you were very strange. I didn't know about these things. But now I respect you and what you have accomplished through hard work and dedication. I am so glad we are friends."

"And I also learned from you," the Discus Thrower said. "I had always been focused on rigorous exercise and believed that difficulties could be resolved through studying and working hard. But now I know that sometimes you need to believe in Tinker Bell, in a different force that you might not be aware of, and that achieving success is often due to a combination of hard work and good luck. And now I know the importance of having friends. I never knew Al and Mike, but they helped me, and Jeff, too. Mostly I am grateful to you, Peter Pan, and I am so glad we are friends."

"We are off into the night," Peter Pan said. "We'll see you again soon."

Tinker Bell swooped down and kissed the Discus Thrower, and said, "Enjoy your first night under the stars." And off they flew, calling out, "Goodnight, Mr. Discus Thrower!"

The Discus Thrower watched them disappear into the summer night and then looked up at the stars and imagined Brother doing the same thing.

The End

The story continues. Use the following pages to sketch views from *your* city.

Meet the Statues

The Discus Thrower, a bronze statue commissioned by Ery Kahaya and sculpted in 1924 by Kostas Dimitriadis, was featured in the 1924 Paris Olympics, winning the Gold Medal in Sculpture. Following the Olympics, the statue was given to the city of New York, and in 1926 it was installed just outside the Metropolitan Museum of Art in Central Park. In 1936, the statue was relocated to Randall's Island and placed at the entrance of the new stadium for the Olympic trials that year. In 1970, the Discus Thrower, which had been vandalized and was missing both an arm and its discus, was moved to storage. There it languished for almost thirty years, until the author, Pinky Keehner, discovered the statue and began planning its restoration. On July 21, 1999, the restored statue was remounted at Randall's Island Park on its marble base designed by McKim, Mead, and White. It is now at the entrance of the park's Icahn Stadium. A replica of the statue was cast in 1927 and still stands near the Panathenaic Stadium in Athens.

The Peter Pan statue was sculpted by Charles Andrew Hefner in 1928 and displayed in the old Paramount Theater in Times Square. In 1975, it was donated to Charles Schurz Park, located at East End Avenue and 87th Street, by Hugh Trumbull Adams. In August 1998, the statue was taken by vandals and tossed into the East River. It was later restored and returned to Charles Schurz Park.

When you are next in New York City, stop by Peter Pan and the Discus Thrower and introduce yourself to your new friends!

Peter Pan, Carl Schurz Park

Peter Pan and the Discus Thrower in the New York City Parks Department's art and antiquities storage facility, August 1998

Pinky Keehner with Peter Pan in the art and antiquities storage facility, August 1998

The Discus Thrower at the Modern Art Foundry in June 1999, with Per von Scheele, athletic director at the Buckley School, and Pinky Keehner

Rededication ceremony for the Discus Thrower in July 1999. From left to right: Karen Cohen, founder of the Randall's Island Park Alliance; Al Oerter, discus thrower and four-time Olympic gold medalist; Pinky Keehner; Grete Waitz, nine-time New York City Marathon winner; Michael Bloomberg, Randall's Island Park Alliance trustee.

Unveiling of the Discus Thrower at his new location in front of Icahn Stadium, April 16, 2024. Photo: Malcolm Pinckney, NYC Parks.

Acknowledgments

Fran Anderson, Eliza Collins, Kay Hedges,
Nancy Neff, Joel Perlman, Nanette Smith,
Jeffrey Spring, Anne Wilson, and Joanne Wilson
For your support

The City of New York's parks & public art

Adrian Benepe, Michael Bloomberg,
Aimee Boden, and Deb Maher
For your kind words of endorsement, which I cherish

Connie Kendrick
*For never saying, "It's done." You were as determined
as I was to make every detail absolutely perfect. It was
a pleasure working with you!*

Cathy Oerter
*For plucking the sentiment of the story from the fairy dust
and transferring it to these pages. What a thrill to partner
with my dear friend who lived this story with me.*

David Fabricant, publisher, Abbeville Press
For telling me, "This book was meant to be read."

Bob Blakely, my husband
For sharing this journey with me

PINKY KEEHNER, a devoted New Yorker, served as vice president of the Randall's Island Park Alliance for 20 years, where she and associates created a state-of-the-art sports facility for New York City kids. Upon finding the life-size bronze Discus Thrower in storage, she made it her mission to restore the statue and return it to its rightful place of honor for all to enjoy.

CATHY OERTER'S love for everything discus began with her husband, Al Oerter, and today she chairs the Al Oerter Foundation and Art of the Olympians. She was an international track and field athlete, majored in art, and found her niche in education to encourage children to use their voices through the arts.

Cathy Oerter (left) and Pinky Keehner, April 16, 2024